Pop Goes the Bubble Trouble

To Bruce,
whose stomach
and joy for life
know no bounds
—G. S.

Pop Goes the Bubble Trouble

By Holly Anna • Illustrated by Genevieve Santos

LITTLE SIMON
New York London Toronto Sydney New Delhi

LITTLE SIMON

An imprint of Simon & Schuster Children's Publishing Division
1230 Avenue of the Americas, New York, New York 10020
First Little Simon paperback edition September 2018
Copyright © 2018 by Simon & Schuster, Inc.
Also available in a Little Simon hardcover edition.
All rights reserved, including the right of reproduction in whole or in part in any form.
LITTLE SIMON is a registered trademark of Simon & Schuster, Inc., and associated colophon is a trademark of Simon & Schuster, Inc. For information about special discounts for bulk purchases, please contact Simon & Schuster Special Sales at 1-866-506-1949 or business@simonandschuster.com. The Simon & Schuster Speakers Bureau can bring authors to your live event. For more information or to book an event contact the Simon & Schuster Speakers Bureau at 1-866-248-3049 or visit our website at www.simonspeakers.com.
Designed by Laura Roode
Manufactured in the United States of America 0818 MTN
2 4 6 8 10 9 7 5 3 1
Library of Congress Cataloging-in-Publication Data
Names: Anna, Holly, author. | Santos, Genevieve, illustrator.
Title: Pop goes the bubble trouble / by Holly Anna ; illustrated by Genevieve Santos.
Description: First Little Simon paperback edition. | New York : Little Simon, 2018.
Series: Daisy Dreamer ; #8 | Summary: "When bubble creatures start disappearing from the World of Make-Believe, Daisy and Posey are on the case!"—Provided by publisher.
Identifiers: LCCN 2018005123 | ISBN 9781534426528 (pbk) | ISBN 9781534426535 (hc)
ISBN 9781534426542 (eBook)
Subjects: | CYAC: Imaginary playmates—Fiction. | Magic—Fiction. | Friendship—Fiction. | BISAC: JUVENILE FICTION / Imagination & Play. | JUVENILE FICTION / Humorous Stories. | JUVENILE FICTION / Readers / Chapter Books.
Classification: LCC PZ7.1.A568 Pop 2018 | DDC [Fic]—dc23
LC record available at https://lccn.loc.gov/2018005123

CONTENTS

☆ CHAPTER ONE ☆

Cleanup on Aisle Nine

SPLAT!

I turn around just in time to see an orange tumble off the tippy-top of the orange pile and sploosh all over the floor.

That's the *third* one in two minutes!

Mom and I are at the grocery store—one of the best places in the world. *Obviously.* Who doesn't love food?

But something keeps knocking the fruit over. And it's not me! I *pinkie swear!*

Just in case, I steer extra clear of the bananas.

KER-SPLAT! KER-SPLUNK!

Across the aisle, two peaches splatter to the floor like juicy yellow fruit bombs. And that's when I see him, sitting on top of the peaches like a little purple monkey with antlers.

"Posey!" I whisper loudly. "What are you doing up there?"

"Shopping!" he shouts with a big sticky grin.

He hops down from the pile in one giant leap, knocking over more fruit. Peach juice drips from his chin.

"These samples are *amazing!*" he says, grabbing an apple and taking a huge bite.

Apples

"Those aren't samples!" I tell him, taking the apple out of his hand. "They are for sale. You have to pay for them first!" *Obviously.*

"Oh," he says, looking a little disappointed. "But I'm hungry!"

I roll my eyes. "You should never go to the grocery store hungry. It makes you want to eat everything!"

Then I swivel the cart around and catch up with Mom. She's moved to the cereal aisle.

"Ooh, Imagination Crunch!" Posey shouts, spying a rainbow-colored cereal box. He throws it into the cart. I quickly take it out and shove it back on the shelf.

"Daisy," Mom questions when I turn back around, "why are there Gooey Roll-Ups in our cart?"

I grab the Gooey Roll-Ups and put those back too. "Sorry, Mom!" I turn and wag my finger at my imaginary friend.

"Posey!" I whisper. "You have to stop!" But he ignores me.

"Can I drive the cart?" he asks.

"No," I say firmly. "Remember, you are invisible, and it'll look like nobody's driving the cart."

Then Posey points at something on the other side of the store.

"Hey, is that Jasmine?" he asks.

I whip around to look for my best friend. "Where?"

And before I can even blink, Posey grabs the shopping cart and zooms down the aisle.

"Wheee!" he shouts.

I race after him and whisper-shout, "Posey, *STOP!*"

But it's too late. *WHAM!*

Posey smashes into a pyramid of canned corn. He looks at me with a sheepish grin. "Cleanup on aisle nine!"

But it's only sort of funny, because now we have to pick up his mess.

"Are you okay?" I ask. "You could have majorly hurt yourself! Or someone else!"

Posey looks down and watches a can of corn roll toward the wall. "Oops. I didn't think about that."

I sigh and begin to pick up the cans and stack them back up.

"It's all right," I say. "I know you didn't mean for it to go badly,

but sometimes you have to listen! Something super fun can become super unfun in a hurry!"

Then my mom comes back from another aisle with a box of spaghetti.

"There you are!" she says as I place the last can back on the top of the display. "Ready to go?"

Posey and I both smile innocently, even though Mom can only see me.

"Yep!" I say. "I am *so* ready to go."

☆ CHAPTER TWO ☆

Presto Prize-o!

"Cash or credit?" the man at the checkout counter asks my mom. Mom pulls out her credit card.

"We're almost finished," I whisper to Posey, but he's gone. I don't see him anywhere. Then I hear it.

RATTLE. RATTLE. RATTLE. Posey is shaking the knobs on the vending machines with toys.

"It's nice to meet you!" he says to one of the machines.

Then he does it to another one. *RATTLE. RATTLE. RATTLE.*

"It's nice to meet you, too!" He introduces himself to every single one.

Of course, the rest of the real world only sees the handles turning . . . by themselves. Customers are mumbling as I race over and cover Posey's hand.

"Posey. What are you doing?" I ask.

He looks up at me with his adorable grin. "I'm introducing myself to

these magnificent machines and the cute little creatures inside them! But none of them are very polite. They haven't said hi back!"

I shake my head in disbelief.

"That's because vending machines and toys can't talk!" I tell him.

Posey's eyebrows shoot up. "What do you mean, they can't talk?"

Posey just doesn't get the real world.

"Because they are not alive," I say, pulling some change out of my pocket. "And you have to pay for them. Watch." I stick the coins into the slot and twist the knob.

Then I open the flap and let the capsule drop into my hand. "Ta-da! Presto prize-o!"

Posey cups his hand over his mouth.

"That's ridiculous!" he exclaims. "In the World of Make-Believe no one takes Bubbles. And the Bubbles all talk!"

I shake my head again and ask, "What are *Bubbles*? Is this another one of your silly tricks?"

Posey put his hands on his hips. "This is not a trick!" he says. "Bubbles are just like the prizes in your vending machines, except they're *real*. And they can talk. I can prove it."

Hmm. Real talking toys? Now this I've got to see!

CHAPTER THREE

SHHWOOP!

"Milk!" I shout, handing a carton of milk to my mom. She puts it in the refrigerator. Mom and I always make a game out of putting the groceries away. Now it's her turn.

"Peanut butter!" she yells, passing a jar of peanut butter to me. I open the cupboard to put it away, and there's Posey, sitting inside the cupboard.

"Can we go upstairs now?" he asks.

"No, not yet," I tell him. "I'm help-ing my mom!" I close the cupboard door and hand Mom a bag of oranges. Then she passes me a jar of spaghetti sauce—and you-know-who is still in the cupboard!

"Can we go up *now*?" Posey asks.

I shove the spaghetti sauce onto the shelf beside him.

"Does it look like I'm done yet?" I say, a little annoyed.

Posey makes a pouty fish face and hops to the floor.

"Okay, I'll wait upstairs," he says.

When I'm done in the kitchen, I scamper upstairs. Posey's waiting, pen in hand.

"You sure took long enough!" he complains.

I frown. "I told you, I had to put the groceries away before I could play. You need to listen to your friends."

Posey lets out a long sigh. "Sorry," he says. "Can we go to the WOM now?"

I nod, and Posey floats to my ceiling and draws a weird-looking door. It looks just like a flap on a vending machine!

"Real kids first!" Posey says.

He lifts the flap open and . . . *SHHHWOOOOOP!* I get sucked up like a vacuum.

"WAHOOO!" I shout as I do a backward loop the loop. Then I slide out of the tube and onto a soft, bouncy floor. *BOING! BOING! BOING!*

I flip-flop around like a fish before I come to a stop. Then I look for Posey, but he doesn't pop out behind me, so I crawl back to the chute and peek inside. He's not in there, either.

"What are you looking for?" asks someone from above me.

I look up and see a big blue hand

floating inside a plastic bubble. The hand has a face and smiles at me.

Did that toy just talk?

Then the talking vending machine bubble toy asks, "May I give you . . . a hand?"

☆ Chapter Four ☆

The City of Vending

The blue hand floats above me in his plastic capsule like a crazy see-through UFO, which stands for "unidentified flying object." *Obviously.*

"You can talk!" I say.

The hand chuckles. "Well, yes. I suppose I can!" he says.

I blush. "Are you a Bubble?" I ask, remembering why Posey brought me here in the first place.

The hand wiggles all his fingers happily. "I am a Bubble, indeed! Call me Luke."

I stand, trying to keep my balance on the springy floor. "Nice to meet you, Luke. I'm Daisy. I'm waiting for my imaginary friend, Posey. He was right behind me and should be here any second."

Luke glances around. "Well, that may not be true," he says.

I bite my bottom lip because I am not fond of iffyness. "What do you mean?" I ask.

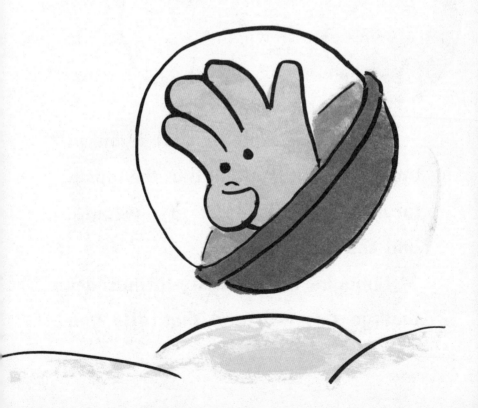

Then Luke explains that I am in the city of Vending and that the topsy-turvy slides may start in one place and end up in another.

I imagine lots of twisty-turny slides that go this way and that. "Do you

think my friend Posey entered Vending
by a different route?"

Luke nods. "Yes, I do," he says.
"Would you like me to help you find
him?"

"Please!" I say.

I take a wibbly-wobbly step on the bouncy floor. I swing my arms to get my balance, but it's no use. I topple and bounce across the ground until I bump into an invisible wall. *It's glass!*

I press my hands against the glass wall as I stand up. Outside I can see the whole wide, dazzling World of Make-Believe! And then I realize something extraordinary. "Am I inside a giant vending machine?"

Luke's eyes light up. "That's why we call it the city of Vending," he says. "We have some of the finest views in the entire WOM."

He's right. I can see for miles. "It's beautiful!" I tell him. "But it's hard to

get around—the floor is so springy."

Luke snaps his fingers. "What you need is a bubble!"

My eyes widen. "Oh, yes please! How do I get one?"

Luke zooms in closer to me.

"It's easy!" he says. "All you have to do is say, 'Bubble, bubble, on the double, keep me safe from any trouble!'"

I repeat the words out loud, and a magical toy capsule surrounds my whole body. Suddenly I'm floating! I lean forward carefully, and I begin to *fly*! *Sweet!* When I lean left, I go left. When I lean right, I go right. It is truly magical.

"Okay," I say, "let's go find my imaginary friend!"

Oh Chute!

The city of Vending is filled with living bubble toys! But it also has shops, restaurants, and playgrounds. The center of Vending has a huge fountain. On the tippy-top of the waterspout there is something bobbing up and down.

"Who could that be?" Luke asks. He points his jellylike finger at the fountain.

I take a closer look. Then I LOL: Laugh. Out. Loud. I know who it is.

"That is my friend Posey!" I cry. Then my silly purple buddy waves as he flips over and over on the water-spout. I roll my eyes and wave back.

Three other Bubbles arrive to help Posey—a shiny red car, a sparkly ring, and a neon-green frog eraser! When they finally get him down, he flies over to me with his rescuers close behind.

The shiny red car has a few words for Posey. "Hmm, I hate to burst your bubble," he says, "but playing in the fountain is against the rules here."

Posey explains that he didn't mean to—it's just where his slide ended. Then the three Bubble friends look at one another and burst out laughing.

"Well, that's just bad design," says the shiny red car. "My name is Carlo. This is Tina, the sparkling ring, and Bop, the glow-in-the-dark eraser."

Posey introduces both of us while I introduce Luke to everyone.

"Hey, would you like to go on the Chutes?" asks Bop. "They are much more fun than riding on the town fountain."

Posey and I never turn down an invitation for fun.

"Of course we want to go!" we say. Then we zip after our new friends.

The Chutes are made up of a whole bunch of different slides. They swirl and spiral around the city like spaghetti noodles. Carlo flies to the top of one and zips down. Then it's my turn. I curve one way and then another. Then I do a triple loop the loop. It's the dizziest!

"AGAIN!" I shout when I come to a stop. But first I have to fix my pigtails. Everyone waits for me. *Obviously.*

"I'm curious," Posey says. "If there are so many slides *inside* Vending, how do you get out?"

This slide question seems to make all these Bubbles uncomfortable. Posey and I give each other a look.

Luckily, Tina breaks the weird silence. "Most Bubbles never leave Vending," she confesses. "Except my best friend, Downy the pom-pom. But that's a strange story."

Well, I love strange stories, I think. "Can you tell us more?" I ask.

The Bubbles look from side to side as if they're worried somebody might be listening in. Then Bop presses his bubble close to mine.

"We're having trouble," he whispers. "Trouble with *holes*."

Chapter Six

Tina's Terrible Tale

"Holes?" Posey whispers—since it seems to be a whispery topic. "What kind of holes?"

Carlo asks us to follow him. He leads us to a huge dark hole in the ground. It is surrounded by yellow caution tape. The hole seems to go down and down forever.

"Hole-y moly!" I whisper.

Posey and I take a step back for fear of falling in.

"This hole appeared without warning," Bop explains.

I notice that Tina looks sad. "Are you okay?" I ask as tenderly as I can.

Then she dabs her eyes with a handkerchief.

"This is the hole my friend Downy fell into," she says, trying not to cry. "And it's all *my fault*! You see, Downy loves to sing. We were playing and she asked me to sing with her, but I wanted to race."

The ring looked down. "I didn't listen to her and zoomed ahead. Downy chased after me. She asked me to slow down, but I still wouldn't listen. When I looked back, the hole was here and Downy was gone."

Tina bursts into tears, and Carlo and Bop try to comfort her.

"Now everyone in Vending is afraid of the holes," Luke says. "Most Bubbles won't even come outside to play anymore."

Posey turns and looks at me gravely. "What do you think is going on, Daisy?" he asks.

I have no idea, but I'm very super-seriously thinking about it. I start to form a hypothesis, which is a fancy word for a guess about what happened. I look at the Bubbles. I look at their city. Then it hits me. We are inside a huge vending machine. *And what do people want from a vending machine?* I ask myself. They want *toys*.

I raise my finger in an aha move to get the group's attention.

"Where I come from," I explain, "kids collect toys from vending machines. I think someone outside of Vending thinks the Bubbles are toys to collect!"

Everyone gasps.

"Why would they do that?" Tina asks. "Toys are not the same thing as friends."

I try to explain my hypothesis. "Well, in the real world, toys are fun and cool! Everybody wants toys. The only difference is that back in the real world, the toys are not alive."

Then everyone starts talking at once because we know we're onto something.

As we're all blabbing away, a new dark hole opens up under Posey and—*shhwoop!*—it swallows him up.

☆ Chapter Seven ☆

The Rescue Crew

"We have to rescue Posey!" I shout, jumping up and down and pointing at the hole. My new friends stare at me in total disbelief.

Then I smile the biggest smile. Mom calls it my *determined* smile. When it flashes across my face, it means I am going to get the job done, no matter what.

"Bubbles, this is the World of Make-Believe," I say. "This is where dreams come true, magic exists, and wonderful adventures are waiting down every hole. Now let's go find Posey and Downy!"

74

As the others cheer I dive directly into the hole and—*whoosh!*—I zoom down the dark slide at lightning speed. I can hear my friends behind me, laughing as they slide down the chute too. My super-speech worked!

Then I slow down. *THWOMP!* I run smack into a heavy vending machine flap. One by one the Bubbles pile into me, and the weight of all five of us pushes open the door.

"Aaaaaaaaah!"

We tumble into a thick forest and spy our first clue in the distance. It's a giant girl . . . and she is holding a Bubble in her hand.

"She has Posey!" I shout. "Let's go!"

We fly after the giant, but we can't keep up with her long strides. Soon she is gone.

"Follow her footprints!" Luke suggests, pointing at the huge marks on the ground. We get right back in gear and track her giant tracks all the way to a frog sitting by a stream.

"Did you see a giant girl pass this way?" Bop asks. The frog ribbits and nods his head.

"Her name is Jean," the frog says. "She's headed back home. It's the giant house over there. You can't miss it."

We say thanks and take off! The crater-size footprints lead to a clearing, where we peek through the bushes and see a giant house. The world is very quiet. Then a small voice drifts in the silence.

"Do you hear singing?" I ask. The Bubbles stay still and listen. It sounds like the voice of a faraway princess.

"I know that voice!" Tina cries. "It's Downy."

Now there is only one thing left that we have to do.

"Follow that melody!" I shout.

☆ CHAPTER EIGHT ☆

A Giant Plan

The beautiful singing is coming from inside the giant house. We fly up to a window and see a giant bed, a giant chair, and a giant picture of Jean. There's no doubt who lives here. Then we see a glass cabinet against the wall. There are two Bubbles in there.

"I see her! I see her!" Tina cries as her bubble bounces with joy.

Uh-oh! I think. *What if Giant Jean hears Tina?* I bump my bubble against Tina's and put my finger to my lips. *"Shhh!"* I shush. "Jean might hear you!"

Then I wave everyone over for a bubble huddle. It's time to hatch a plan. *Obviously.*

"Here's what we're going to do," I say. "We wait for Jean to go to sleep. Then we fly under the door. And remember, we have to be super-duper quiet because giant ears can hear *everything.* Then we sneak over to the cabinet and free Downy and Posey. Got it?"

Everyone gives me an A-OK.

"And one more thing!" I add. "We need to be sneaky, so let's each pick a hiding place in case Jean wakes up."

There are great hiding places in a giant house: behind the curtains, under the rug, beside the chair, behind the sofa, even inside the pitcher on the table.

"I'll hide under the rug!" calls someone from behind me. He has a familiar voice.

I spin around and see Posey!

"What are you doing here?" I cry. "We just made a plan to save you!"

He laughs. "I know. It looked fun, so I wanted to help! I drew a door with my pen and snuck right out of the giant's house!"

"Posey," I say with a laugh, "you already saved yourself. Now can we borrow your pen to draw a door and free Downy?"

Posey begins to search his fur, looking for the pen.

Then he gives me a confused look, and I know exactly what happened. "You lost your pen, didn't you?"

He shrugs. "I didn't think I'd need it again."

I smack my hand against my forehead. "Okay, Bubble Brigade. It's back to plan A."

☆ Chapter Nine ☆

Bubble Trouble

Honk-shoo! Honk-shoo!

The Jolly Jean Giant is snoring her head off. Let the rescue mission begin! We charge under the door, and everyone gets inside.

As we float across the room I realize that Posey is missing. Then I notice a lump under the rug, and it's moving. *That crazy Posey! He hid under the*

rug and now he's lost. Maybe we will still have to save him after all.

The rest of us fly to the cabinet and land on its great big handle. I look at Luke and say, "Hey, remember when you asked if you could give me a hand? We could use one now."

Luke nods, and then he pops open his bubble. With his handy head, he grabs the handle and opens the cabinet.

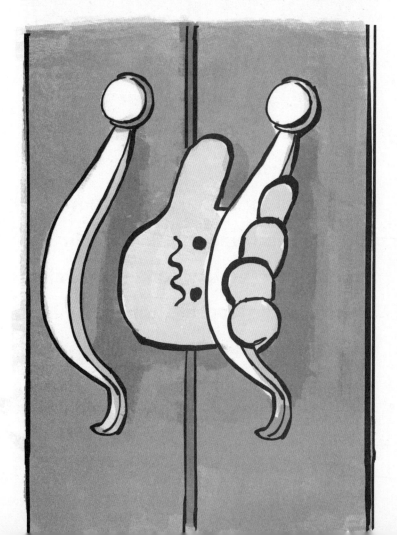

Downy lets out a cheer song that rings through the room. Tina joins in with another sweet melody.

I am all for happy friends, but these Bubbles are being a little too loud. No one but me notices that Jean's giant snoring has stopped. Instead, we hear the stomp of footsteps! And I'm pretty sure we're all in big bubble trouble. *Obviously.*

Giant Jean storms into the room and—*wow*—everything about her looks like a normal eight-year-old girl. She has long brown hair, navy leggings, a striped top, and a pink cardigan. The only tiny difference is, she's *ginormous*.

"WHO'S THERE?" she booms.

The Bubbles scatter and hide, but Downy and I freeze right in place.

"WAIT! WAIT!" Jean the giant cries. "WAIT, DOWNY, PLEASE DON'T LEAVE! YOU'RE MY ONLY FRIEND!"

My heart softens a little when Jean uses the word "friend." We thought we were saving Downy. Maybe we were wrong!

Then Downy flies up to Jean. "Did you hear me singing?" she asks.

Jean nods. It is like watching a mountain move its head up and down.

"It was a sad song because I miss my home and my other friends," Downy says.

Jean steps back in surprise. Her voice softens. "I thought you liked it here. I thought you liked me. Didn't we have fun?"

Downy frowns, and I can feel my heart go all Jell-O.

"We *did* have fun, and I *am* your friend," Downy explains.

The Bubble floats next to Jean. "But you still aren't listening, and friends should always listen. So hear me now: I am ready to go home."

Jean hangs her head sadly. "All I wanted was to have a friend. I'm *so* sorry!" She covers her face with her hands, and giant tears spill to the floor.

And now I feel bad for Jean because she doesn't look like a giant at all anymore. She looks like a kid who made a mistake. *She is truly sorry*, I think. She tried to make friends the wrong way.

Then one by one the Bubbles come out of their hiding places. They fly up to Jean, but they don't look mad at all. In fact, they look relaxed and even laugh a little. That helps Jean calm down too.

And while everyone else is almost happily ever after, Posey chooses that very moment to blast out from under the rug.

"I FOUND IT!" he cries. And now it's all eyes off Miss Waterworks and all eyes on Posey. My imaginary friend

has a knack for drawing attention to himself.

"Found WHAT?" I ask.

"I found my pen!" he says, waving it in the air.

I look at his pen, and it suddenly gives me a *giant* idea.

CHAPTER TEN

The Friendship Door

"Posey, can I borrow your pen?" I ask.

Posey looks at his pen, then tosses it right to me. I draw a Bubble-size door on the wall in Jean's house. Then I write FRIENDSHIP DOOR on it.

"Attention, everyone," I cheer. "This is the friendship door. It opens both ways. On one side is Vending, where the Bubbles live. On the other side is, well . . . here at Jean's house. Now you can visit each other whenever you want—and you can go home whenever you want too!"

Posey cracks open the door, and the Bubbles wave good-bye to Jean before sliding through. The last ones left are Tina, Downy, Posey, and me.

Downy flies up to Jean and nuzzles against her cheek. Then Downy sings in a beautiful voice, "Do not worry. Don't you fret. We'll be back tomorrow, you bet. Because you are my truly giant friend."

Jean smiles and waves good-bye.

When Tina and Downy have gone, Posey and I leap through the friend-ship door last. As I fall through space, I hear Mom calling my name in the distance. My bubble begins to dissolve.

"Good-bye, Bubble friends!" I call out. And then I drift toward home and land gently on top of my bed just as Mom opens the door.

"There you are, Daisy Dreamer!" Mom says. She moves her hands behind her back. "I got you a special something," she says. "Pick a hand!"

Oooh, I *love* this game! I point to her left hand.

"Ta-da!" she says.

It's a vending machine bubble! And inside is a shiny unicorn sticker. I pluck it out of her hand.

"Oh, Mom, I love it," I say. "Thank you!"

She gives me a hug. "I saw you admiring it at the store today, so I snuck back and got you one for being so helpful."

Wait, does Mom know I helped the Bubbles today?

"Helpful?" I repeat uncertainly.

Mom laughs. "Yes!" she says. "For helping me with the shopping and putting away the groceries!"

"Oooh," I say, sighing with *giant* relief. "Anytime, Mom!" Then I admire my new sticker. And I know just where I'm going to bring it—back to the World of Make-Believe with Posey and all my Bubble friends!

Check out Daisy Dreamer's next adventure!

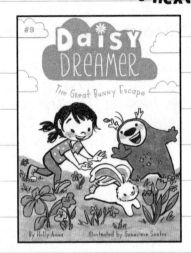

#9
Daisy Dreamer
The Great Bunny Escape

By Holly Anna   Illustrated by Genevieve Santos

BRRRING!

The school bell rings, and my best friends, Lily and Jasmine, and I make a mad dash for the playground. It's recess! Our favorite time of the day. *Obviously.*

Excerpt from *The Great Bunny Escape*

We hit the blacktop and run straight to the Hideout—our top secret hiding spot under the slide.

It's the best place for telling secrets because it keeps all the snoopy-snoops like Gabby Gaburp and Carol Rattinger out.

Today Lily has a *huge* secret. I can tell because she always twirls her hair around her finger when she's hiding something. And she's been twirling her hair ALL. DAY. LONG.

"Spill, Lil!" I say as soon as we're safe inside the Hideout.

"Let's make extra sure the coast

is clear first," Lily says. So Jasmine double-checks the entry to make sure Carol and Gabby aren't spying on us. You can never be too careful when it comes to those two girls. They want to know *everything* about *everyone.*

"All clear!" Jasmine calls.

"Okay," Lily begins. "You may have already guessed I have a secret to tell, and I also have a favor to ask."

That sounds like a double-dog secret! I think, scootching closer to her side. And I am double-dog interested.

Excerpt from *The Great Bunny Escape*